A BIT LOST

"Thus we never see the true State of our Condition, till it is illustrated to us by its Contraries; nor know how to value what we enjoy, but by the want of it."
ROBINSON CRUSOE, Daniel Defoe

To Mum and Dad xx

This edition published 2010 by Walker Books Ltd
87 Vauxhall Walk, London SE11 5HJ

10 9 8 7 6 5 4 3 2

© 2009, 2010 Chris Haughton

Published by arrangement with Borim Press, Korea

The right of Chris Haughton to be identified as author/illustrator of this work has been asserted by him in accordance with the Copyright, Designs and Patents Act 1988

This book has been typeset in A Bit Lost

Printed in Italy

British Library Cataloguing in Publication Data:
a catalogue record for this book is available from the British Library

ISBN 978-1-4063-2746-5

www.walker.co.uk

WALKER BOOKS
AND SUBSIDIARIES
LONDON · BOSTON · SYDNEY · AUCKLAND

A BIT LOST

CHRIS HAUGHTON

Uh-oh!

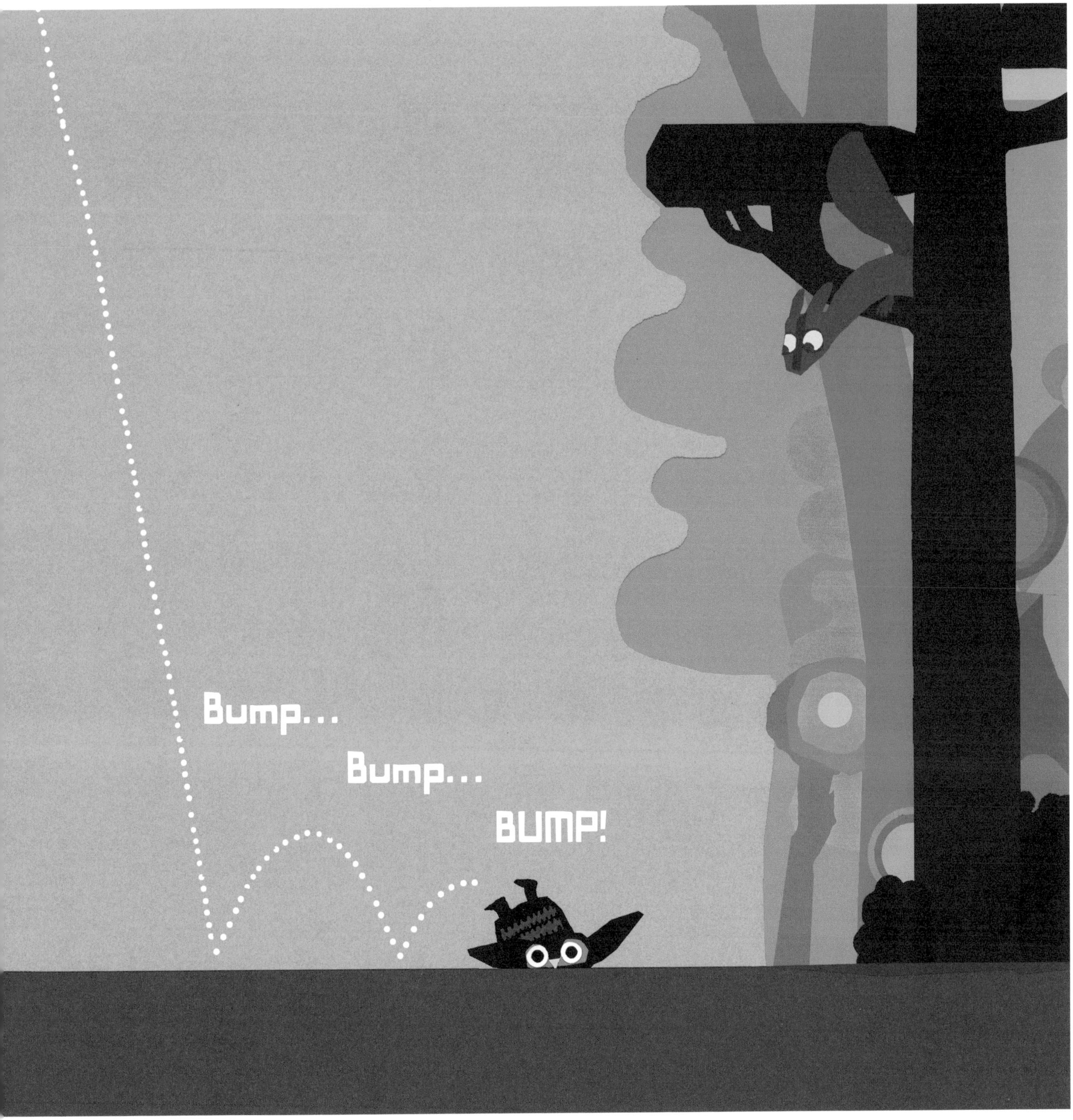

Bump...

Bump...

BUMP!

"Are you OK?"
asked Squirrel.
"I'm lost," said Little Owl.
"Where's my mummy?"

"Don't worry, little friend.
I'll find your mummy.
What does she
look like?"

"My mummy is
VERY BIG. Like THIS!"
said Little Owl.

"Yes! Yes!
I know! I know!"
said Squirrel.
"Follow me...

Here she is.
Here's your mummy!"

"No! No!" said Little Owl.
"That's not my mummy.
My mummy has POINTY EARS.
Like THIS!"

"Yes! Yes!
I know! I know!"
said Squirrel.
"Follow me...

Here she is.
Here's your mummy!"

"No! No!" said Little Owl.
"That's not my mummy.
My mummy has BIG EYES.
Like THIS!"

"Yes! Yes!
I know! I know!"
said Squirrel.
"Follow me...

Here she is.
Here's your mummy!"

"No," said Little Owl.
"That's not my mummy either."

"Wait a minute," said Frog.
"I know your mummy...

Follow me. Your mummy's
looking everywhere
for you.

Is this your mummy?"

"Yes! Yes!
Here she is!
Here's my
mummy."

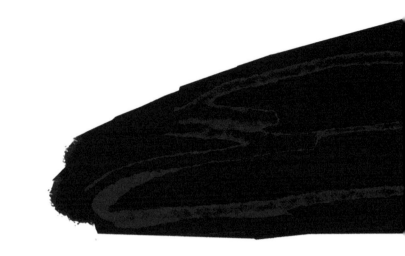

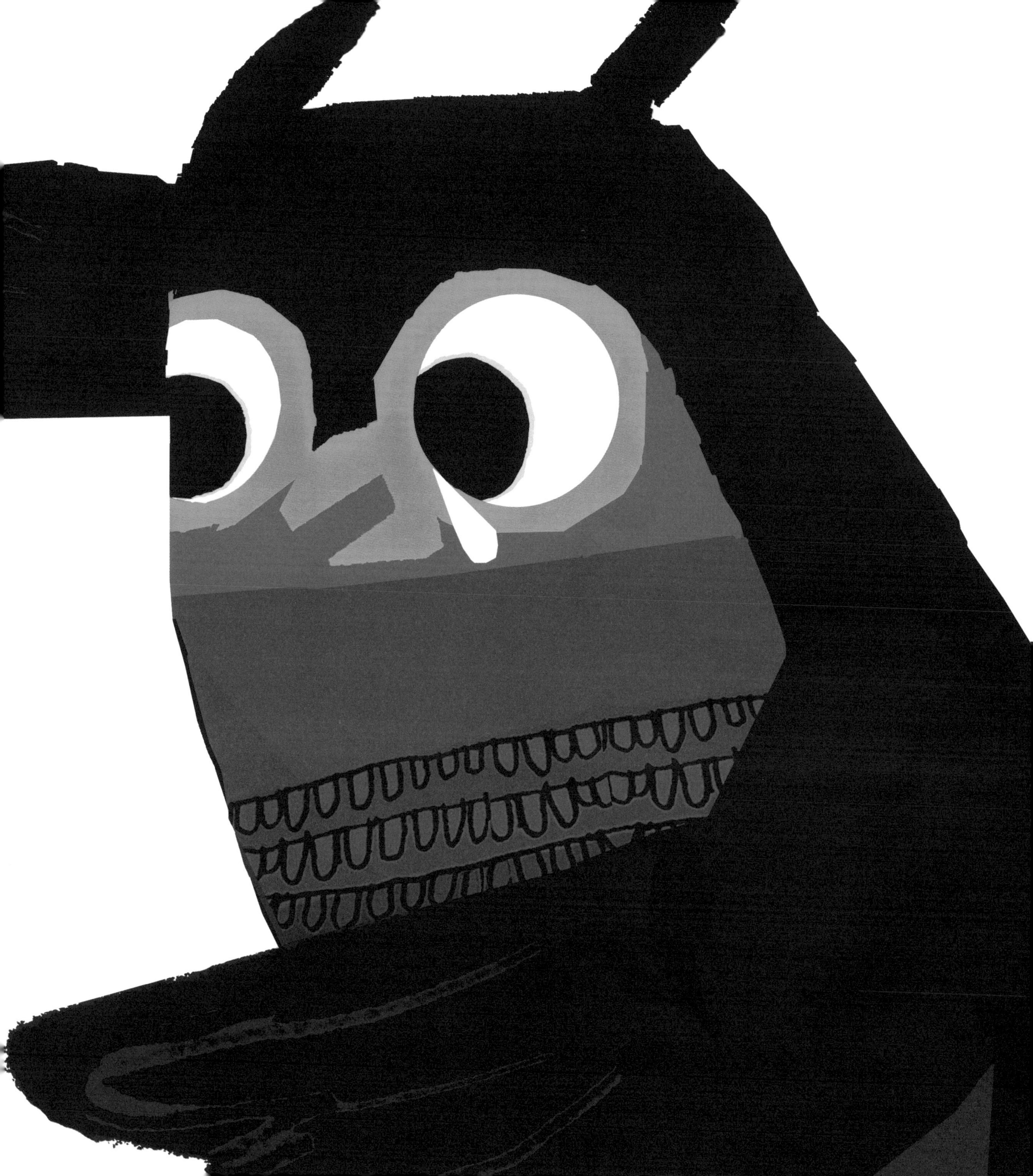

"Oh, thank you,"
said Mummy Owl.
"Why don't you come
up to our nest for
some biscuits?"

"Yes, please,"
said Squirrel. "Biscuits
are our favourite thing."